DR. DRABBLE, GENIUS INVENTOR
Dr. Drabble's Incredible Identical Robot Innovation
Dr. Drabble's Phenomenal Antigravity Dust Machine
Dr. Drabble's Remarkable Underwater Breathing Pills
Dr. Drabble's Astounding Musical Mesmerizer
Dr. Drabble's Spectacular Shrinker- Enlarger
Dr. Drabble's Amazing Invisibility Mirror
Dr. Drabble's Wondrous Weather Dispenser
Dr. Drabble's Fantastic Fanfaring Finder

# DR. DRABBLE'S
# AMAZING INVISIBILITY
# MIRROR

*Written by*
**Sigmund Brouwer and Wayne Davidson**
*Illustrated by*
**Bill Bell**

**VICTOR BOOKS**®
A DIVISION OF SCRIPTURE PRESS PUBLICATIONS INC.
USA CANADA ENGLAND

To *Dustin
and Krista*

ISBN: 0-89693-970-7

© 1992 SP Publications, Inc. All
rights reserved.

VICTOR BOOKS
A division of SP Publications, Inc.
Wheaton, Illinois 60187

PJ and Chelsea were in Japan with
their missionary parents. All of them
traveled around the world on the Bril-
liant All-in-One Traveling Apparatus
that belonged to a genius inventor
named Dr. Drabble.

Chelsea and PJ were fighting over a
piece of licorice in Dr. Drabble's
laboratory.

"I say we share this licorice half and
half," PJ said.

"But I'm hungrier than you are,"
Chelsea said. She pulled hard.

Before PJ could reply, *SNAP,* the
licorice broke in two.

Chelsea fell backward, right into Dr.
Drabble's old-fashioned mirror.

PJ waited for the crash of breaking
glass.

But there was no crash. And when
he opened his eyes, there was no Chelsea, and the mirror was still there.

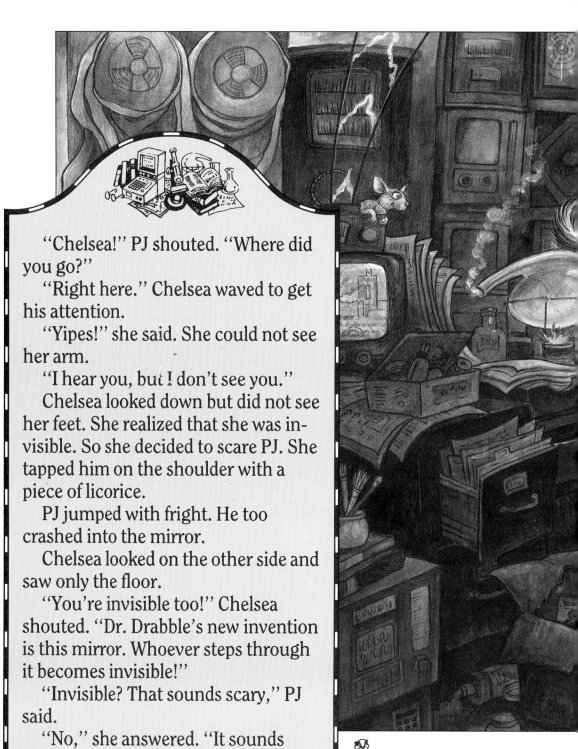

"Chelsea!" PJ shouted. "Where did you go?"

"Right here." Chelsea waved to get his attention.

"Yipes!" she said. She could not see her arm.

"I hear you, but I don't see you."

Chelsea looked down but did not see her feet. She realized that she was invisible. So she decided to scare PJ. She tapped him on the shoulder with a piece of licorice.

PJ jumped with fright. He too crashed into the mirror.

Chelsea looked on the other side and saw only the floor.

"You're invisible too!" Chelsea shouted. "Dr. Drabble's new invention is this mirror. Whoever steps through it becomes invisible!"

"Invisible? That sounds scary," PJ said.

"No," she answered. "It sounds *fun!*"

"Let's play a joke on Arnie," Chelsea suggested. Arnie Clodbuckle was Dr. Drabble's assistant.

They knocked on Arnie's door.

"Who is it?" Arnie called out.

"Shhh!" Chelsea whispered to PJ. "When he opens the door we can sneak in."

Arnie opened the door. "Who is it?" Chelsea pulled PJ inside.

When Arnie turned around, he saw that his teddy bear was flying!

Actually, Chelsea was holding it, but since she was invisible, the teddy bear really seemed to fly.

PJ said in a deep voice, "Arnie, why did you take all the covers last night? How can a teddy bear sleep if he is cold?"

"Aaaaaaaak!" Arnie jumped up on his chair. "I'm very sorry. I'll never hog the covers again."

PJ and Chelsea giggled.

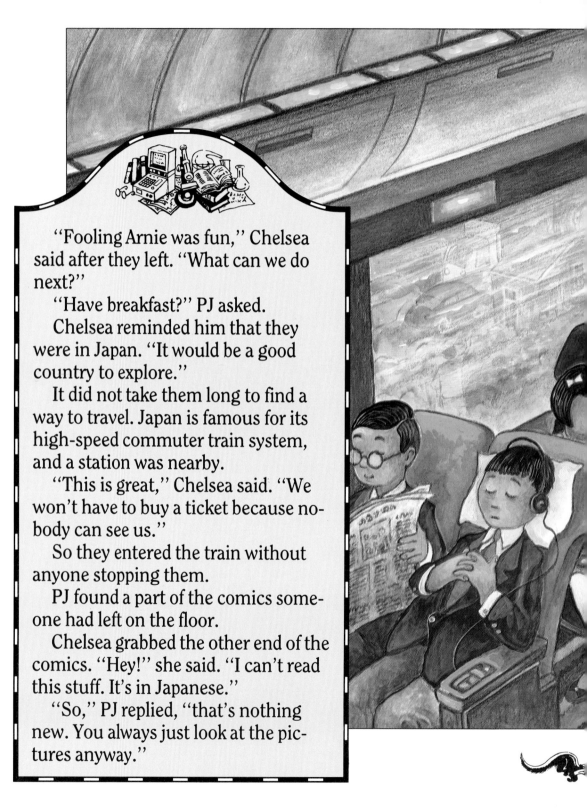

"Fooling Arnie was fun," Chelsea said after they left. "What can we do next?"

"Have breakfast?" PJ asked.

Chelsea reminded him that they were in Japan. "It would be a good country to explore."

It did not take them long to find a way to travel. Japan is famous for its high-speed commuter train system, and a station was nearby.

"This is great," Chelsea said. "We won't have to buy a ticket because nobody can see us."

So they entered the train without anyone stopping them.

PJ found a part of the comics someone had left on the floor.

Chelsea grabbed the other end of the comics. "Hey!" she said. "I can't read this stuff. It's in Japanese."

"So," PJ replied, "that's nothing new. You always just look at the pictures anyway."

Chelsea became bored. She looked out the window of the train.

"Look!" she said. "An amusement park! We'll get off at the next stop."

It was very easy for PJ and Chelsea to get inside the amusement park. They just walked in and began to have fun.

First they found an empty seat on the ferris wheel and rode on it three times. Then they went inside the magic house of mirrors, but soon discovered that it was boring because they couldn't see themselves.

They moved through the park and next found the bumper cars.

"It is so fun being invisible," Chelsea told PJ. "Nobody can see us driving this, and we can hit them when they don't expect it!"

After bumper cars, they went to the roller coaster.

Because they were invisible, they could stay on the roller coaster for many rides. All they had to do was switch seats whenever it looked like someone might sit on them.

From the top of the roller coaster on their last ride, they noticed the nearby zoo.

"Oh!" Chelsea exclaimed. "The zoo would be a perfect place to be invisible. Think of all the animals we could see up close."

Before PJ could reply, the people in front of them spilled popcorn. It covered PJ and Chelsea like snow, and they had to quickly brush it off before anyone noticed them.

"That was too close," Chelsea said as the roller coaster stopped. "If someone saw us, we might have had to pay for this ride. Let's go to the zoo right away."

The children happily entered the zoo without tickets.

Once inside, their fun continued.

They were able to get very close to many different kinds of animals.

In the monkey cage, they helped peel bananas. They shelled peanuts and fed some surprised elephants.

But they had the most fun by tricking people who were watching the baby hippopotamus.

PJ and Chelsea stood right beside the baby hippopotamus. Of course, no one saw them there. When it yawned, one kid watching said, "Look at the size of *that* mouth."

PJ pretended the baby hippo was speaking and quickly said to the kid in a deep voice, "Your mouth isn't so small either."

After that, PJ and Chelsea decided to visit the bears.

They noticed that the zookeeper was cleaning the outside area where the bears sometimes sat in the sun.

"Hurry," Chelsea said, "we can sneak in while the door is open and get a closer look."

"Are you sure that's a good idea?"

"Of course. The bear can't see us."

The children entered, but soon discovered that the bear did not have to see them to know they were there.

The bear growled.

"Oh no," Chelsea remembered. "Bears can smell people."

The bear growled again and moved toward them.

"Run!" PJ shouted. "Get to a tree before he finds us!"

PJ and Chelsea climbed the tree as fast as they could.

"Help! Help!" they shouted as the bear reached upward. "Help!"

"That's strange," the zookeeper said when he heard them, "I didn't know trees could speak English."

"It's not a tree! It's us! We're invisible!" PJ called. "Please help!"

"Who?"

"Us! Us!" they shouted.

The zookeeper scratched his head. "Mmm. An *us*. Must be a new animal to the zoo."

"No," Chelsea cried. "We're invisible children who snuck into the zoo."

"You mean you didn't pay?"

"Yes. I mean no," PJ cried louder. "Nobody could see us, so we thought it would be okay."

"Wait here," the zookeeper replied. "I have a way of making you visible. Then I can help."

The zookeeper returned with hats and sunglasses, which, of course, had not fallen through Dr. Drabble's Amazing Invisibility Mirror.

"Put these on," he instructed. "That way I can see you and help you down."

He led the bear away from the tree, and when he returned, PJ and Chelsea were nearly to the ground.

"Follow me," the zookeeper said as he lifted the children safely to the ground. "We must now call your parents and tell them everything. Even the part about sneaking into the zoo without paying."

PJ and Chelsea began to realize that they had been dishonest.

"We knew it was stealing," PJ moaned. "And God says that's wrong."

"I know," Chelsea agreed. "But it seemed so fun, I wanted to pretend it was okay."

When they got back to the ship, Dr. Drabble sent them through the Amazing Invisibility Mirror from the other side and they were visible again. PJ and Chelsea confessed everything they had done.

They explained how they had taken a train ride without paying, how they had gone into the amusement park without paying, and how they had snuck into the zoo without paying.

"We know it was wrong," Chelsea said. "We're sorry."

"Sorry enough to go back and pay for it all?" Mom asked.

"Ouch," PJ said. He looked at Chelsea. "We'll have to empty our piggy banks."

When they broke them open, they found nothing.

"All our money is gone!"

"No," Arnie laughed. "Invisible. Do you like *my* joke on *you?*"